The Story of Luvee Bunny

By Peter Volkmann

Copyright © 2018 Peter Volkmann

All rights reserved.

ISBN-13: 978-1-7239-9718-1

ACKNOWLEDGMENTS

The Luvee Bunny concept was one of many gifts of my recovery that began on my first day of recovery, September 2, 1995. I would like to recognize the efforts of my family and friends for their encouragement and support during the creation of Luvee Bunny. Thank you to my wife Layne for her persistence and editing…and editing…and editing that made this book happen. Thanks to my daughter Jaycee in providing your artistic talents that brought the Luvee Bunny story to life. Thank you to my son, Peter, who engineered the final draft to perfection. Thanks to my mom, Jan, who gave the mother's touch that was needed in the story. Every recommendation was perfect. Thank you to my friend, Robby Rothfeld, for your steadfast mentorship and encouragement throughout the process. This story is a collaboration of compassion and hope from special people who demonstrate the good in the world every day. I could not have done this without all of you.

1. LUVEE BUNNY

Once upon a time, a long time ago, there was the story of Peter Rabbit, a wily and wonderful rabbit if there was ever one. But have you heard the story about his lifelong bunny wife, Luvee Bunny?

You haven't heard? Oh, my, I must tell you then. It is a wonderful story about another wonderful bunny.

I'll begin with Peter Rabbit. Peter became famous in Bunnyland. He was a friend to everyone, and he helped many other rabbits when they encountered tough times. His family was so proud of all he had done in the past, and proud of the bright future ahead.

He chose not to live the usual life like so many other bunnies. For instance, he went out in the daytime when it was risky instead of playing at night when it was safer from dangerous animals. He would always explore into unfamiliar pastures which was risky because of the potential dangers. Peter would always return with exciting bunny stories of what he had experienced. Some bunnies thought he was crazy to venture into unknown pastures, and not stay in a predictable, safe pasture. Peter lived the way he wanted.

One day Peter met Luvee Bunny. Luvee Bunny was the cutest brown bunny who charmed any animal she met. Her friendly personality would bring a smile to all who knew her. She was a few years younger than Peter and was amazed that he wanted to spend time with her. In fact,

Luvee Bunny still wasn't allowed to venture out into other pastures, while Peter had been venturing about for some time. Luvee Bunny was scared of the unknown pastures. She lacked the confidence to step out beyond the sight of home. Thus Luvee Bunny thought she was too young and boring for him.

Luvee Bunny's family was amazed of the friendship between Luvee and Peter. They were happy that Luvee Bunny had as good a friend as Peter, who was indeed a special and wonderful rabbit.

Luvee Bunny and Peter would go out into the pasture at night and laugh and play and have so much fun. Everyone in Bunnyland smiled when they saw the two together. They were as fun as a couple of clowns and as close as two bunnies could get and were always laughing together.

One day Peter asked Luvee Bunny to play in the pasture during the daytime.

Luvee Bunny exclaimed, "No, I can't!"

"Why not, Luvee Bunny?" Peter asked.

Luvee Bunny replied, "Everybody says it's too unsafe for bunnies. I'm a smaller bunny, which means I can really get hurt. There are too many bunnies that get hurt around here. Anyways, my mother and father say that I should only go out into the safety of darkness. They warn me to never leave sight of our pasture, especially in the daylight. They don't want me to get hurt. They said it's too risky to take the chance."

Peter thought for a moment, "That risky part of life is a wonderful experience. There are some mean animals, but when you confront them and talk, well, they're just not as mean as you'd think. You merely have to learn how to protect yourself. I'll teach you. You are strong, Luvee Bunny, stronger than you think, and you can handle the dangers. You have bunny wisdom and bunny strength. Come with me and we can see so much beauty in life."

Luvee Bunny wanted so desperately to go. "But if I go, my mother and father will worry. They take good care of me and I don't want them to worry about me. Peter, you are so much smarter and braver than I will ever be. That's why you can go and I can't. I would only be a burden in your journeys."

Peter, feeling very sad, "Luvee Bunny, I am a bunny like all others, I am no different. I hope someday you will realize that you can develop the courage to go out and experience other pastures. Only you can decide the steps you take in life. I know that I will always love you and want to go to other pastures with you."

He paused for a moment and took a deep breath before continuing. "Now, I must continue on my journeys into other pastures. I find my bunny journey's into unknown pastures is what makes my life wondrous. I hope to return to this pasture from time to time, and I will always come to see you. While I travel, I will think of you always. Goodbye, Luvee Bunny. I will miss you."

He turned to go, but then turned back and said, "While I am away, if you need someone because you feel you are confused, go to the Big Ol' Oak Tree. The Wise Ol' Owl who lives there will share life's truths with you. Go only when you are ready to hear the truth about everything, including yourself. Otherwise you will be wasting your time, and the Owl's advice will be of no use to you."

With those words said, off Peter went.

Luvee Bunny felt alone and sad. She knew she would miss Peter Rabbit. She didn't know if she had made the correct decision.

Luvee Bunny's mother and father watched over her well. Their stories of past bunny tragedies continued to frighten her, making her scared of the future. She became afraid to make decisions. So, she lived her life afraid of any adventure.

Time passed. Luvee Bunny lived in the same pasture. Her family was always nearby taking care of her. But soon, as her friends grew up, they explored the other pastures. Luvee Bunny wished she could go with them, especially when she heard so many bunny stories. Her parent's supervision always cautioned her, and she could not get out from under their influence.

As for Peter Rabbit, he did come back from time to time. He would always stop by and say hello. He did not again ask Luvee Bunny to go with him on his journeys knowing she would not go. Sometimes he would ask her if she had visited the Wise Ol' Owl, but each time she would shake her head no, and say, "I guess I am not ready."

But, as time went on, Peter's stops became less frequent. Luvee Bunny couldn't bear to listen to any more stories of her friends' adventures to other pastures. She stayed in her burrow, hardly ate, and became weaker. She was unhappy with her life. She didn't want to live feeling unhappy but she didn't know how to change her life. Her family continued their stance about staying in their own pasture, even though they knew Luvee Bunny needed more. They didn't understand that for Luvee Bunny, simply staying put was not the right answer for her life. They just sighed and protected her, as parents sometimes do.

Oh, how sad Luvee Bunny was! She missed the love she and Peter had shared. She missed him terribly. Life was passing by in her predictable, safe burrow hole.

Yet she never forgot Peter's advice about the Ol' Oak Tree. She feared talking to the Wise Ol' Owl! She struggled with her fears about talking.

2. THE WISE OL' OWL

The day finally came when Luvee Bunny knew her life would pass her by unless she had the courage to face her feelings and visit the Wise Ol' Owl. She realized she had nothing to lose by facing up to all the fears that stopped her from talking to the Wise Ol' Owl. She recognized her parents best intentions were not a replacement for her own desires and her own courage.

One early morning as the sun rose, Luvee Bunny hopped to the Ol' Oak Tree. She sat there and waited and finally heard a "Whoo" up top in the tree.

At first Luvee Bunny was scared. Using all of her courage she replied, "It's just me, Luvee Bunny."

"Why hello there," a friendly voice answered back. It was not the intimidating voice Luvee Bunny imagined would come from an old and wise creature.

"Hello Mr. Wise Ol' Owl," Luvee Bunny said in a small voice. "Could you please come out of your tree and talk to me?"

"Of course, I can," the owl said. Suddenly Luvee Bunny saw him hop out of a hole in the top of the tree and perch on a branch. The owl looked down at her with huge eyes seeming to glow straight at her. "I know why you have come here," he said. "You are looking for answers about your life."

Luvee Bunny was surprised. "Why yes! How did you know?"

The owl spoke calmly and sweetly as he said, "From up here in the tree, with the special vision we owls have, I can see all that happens in many different pastures, all at once. And I have noticed you, Luvee Bunny. You have remained alone in your burrow and have not taken any journeys. I have seen so many other bunnies go far into other pastures, but never you."

Luvee Bunny's eyes filled with tears as she said, "You see much more being an owl. I wish I was you. I don't like myself. I don't like being a bunny. I don't like being afraid. I want to see all those other pastures like everyone else does. But I'm just scared. All my life, my parents have told me that it's too risky."

The owl nodded thoughtfully for a moment and said, "I am who I am, and you are who you are. Each of us has our own views of pastures. You can never see pastures the way I do, and yet,

I will never see pastures the way you do. We always learn from each other's experiences in life."

"I never would think that you learn from bunny stories. But what about the risks?" asked Luvee Bunny. "I'm so scared."

The Wise Ol' Owl replied, "Every creature lives with the risks of life. If we don't take risks, how can we grow? It can be scary to go into new pastures. But if you never go, you'll miss some of the most beautiful sights. Some sights are so beautiful that you could never imagine. And there are many good animals that will be your friend."

The Wise Ol' Owl paused for a moment and looked deeper into Luvee Bunny 's eyes.

"You are in control of your decisions," he said. "And the choices are up to you. Eventually you will decide when it's time for you to explore new pastures. You will decide when the time has come and the risks are worth it. You will make the right decision at the right time. It will happen naturally one step at a time."

"When you do go, you may find some pastures are easy to navigate and filled with fine things to eat. Or you may encounter hard times, when the land is difficult to travel, food is scarce, and other animals threaten you. The most important thing you must learn is not to fear the future. For you will take each pasture as it comes, and find the right course for yourself."

Luvee Bunny nodded her little head slowly, and then she said, "But what about my family? They will worry."

The owl smiled. "Your family loves you and understands that all bunnies desire bunny stories. Even though we rely on each other, we are all individuals who experience life our own way. Your family will never break away from you and you will never break away from your family. But, eventually we each must live our own life."

"I am a girl, and weak, and don't have the strength," Luvee Bunny said.

The owl possessed much patience, as all who will help others must do. "Luvee Bunny, oh but you do," he said. "It does not matter whether you are a girl or a boy, or whether you are large or small. But you must make the proper steps to go forward in your life. That decision to go is up to you."

The Wise Ol' Owl cleared his throat, and spoke slowly with great passion. "You must first realize that you have the strength and wisdom to explore other pastures. Until you do, you may stay here with me. During this time, you will exercise and eat properly. You will grow stronger, inside and out. I will protect you while you are here. I will let your parents know that you are with me. You'll have nothing to worry about. You can concentrate on asking me questions and getting ready to take your first steps to begin your first bunny journey in life."

Luvee Bunny looked at the owl and nodded without saying a word.

Hours turned into days and days turned into weeks for Luvee Bunny as she stayed near the Ol' Oak Tree. She felt strength growing within her as she realized that her fears were small, and her untapped strengths were large.

She saw many hours of daylight for the first time since she could remember. She recognized there is much more to see during the day time. She understood her family was not mad because she was away. She sometimes asked the Wise Ol' Owl a question or two about the world. He always had an answer that made her understand the only way to really know what was out there was to go and see the pastures for herself.

The day came when she truly felt the desire to explore other pastures. Luvee Bunny knew what she wanted more than anything. Luvee Bunny wanted to find Peter.

"Wise Ol' Owl," Luvee Bunny said, "I have recognized that I am stronger and I think I am ready to explore other pastures. I have decided to find Peter Rabbit. I can never thank you enough for giving me the strength and the wisdom to seek a full life."

The owl smiled. "I am glad to hear this, Luvee Bunny. You have always possessed strength and wisdom to deal with what the future brings. You have grown as you should."

"Now that you have learned how wonderful you are, your family will be waiting for you when you return with your first bunny story. You will experience pastures that are truly beyond description. Most importantly, you will find whatever is waiting for you. All it takes is your first step. Goodbye my lovely, strong friend."

Luvee Bunny smiled as a tear rolled from the

corner of one eye. "Goodbye," she simply said, and hopped off to seek her future.

3. TWELVE STEPS

Luvee Bunny began her journey to pastures beyond bunny sight for the first time. It didn't take long before she began to doubt herself, and soon she was once again scared. She understood she needed to apply the steps she learned and she remembered Wise Ol' Owl's lessons of bunny wisdom.

She thought "One never knows what's ahead." Then she remembered what Wise Ol' Owl said when she'd first met him weeks ago. "The most important thing is that you must learn not to fear the future. For you will take each pasture as it comes and find the right course for yourself."

Luvee Bunny kept hopping forward.

She looked back to her pasture from time to time, and couldn't help feeling sad leaving her home. She remembered both good and bad memories that she would keep with her always. She knew her memories would never go away.

As she hopped along, she thought while memories are fine, show would now be creating her own stories from her own experiences out in the world. She'd have those stories to tell when she returned to her own pasture. Her dreams were happening right now.

Imagine, Luvee Bunny was looking forward to the future! She understood every bunny had the opportunity to experience the unknown. Some bunnies would choose to remain in their own familiar, safe pasture. Some would not. There is no right way or wrong way to live a bunny life. She absolutely knew her choices would not be made out of fear.

Luvee Bunny had made her choice: to explore the unknown of life. She was determined to follow through and find many other pastures.

"Goodbye old pasture," Luvee Bunny said out loud, as she looked back for the last time. She was about to go down the other side of a big hill, and the pasture would be out of bunny sight. "Home will always be here and it will always be in my heart. Now I must move on in my life to other pastures."

Luvee Bunny paused, and then she spoke aloud. "I want to find Peter!"

With the decision to find Peter, Luvee Bunny hopped from one pasture to another. She noted it had been a long but joyous first day away from her home. Her journey filled her with pride and freedom that she'd always longed for. Now it was time to find rest, and soon look for shelter. She stopped along a beautiful lake that reflected all there was to see. The colors were more beautiful than any pasture she had seen.

She smelled the freshness of the water. She heard the soothing sound of water moving on the shore in little ripples. Luvee Bunny could not remember the last time she took a moment to notice the beauty of the world. She looked at herself in the still blue water, and for the first time, she felt that she was a wonderful bunny. She was proud that she had taken the big step that would change her life.

Just then she heard a snap of a twig. Luvee Bunny froze. She remembered that all day she had not seen another animal up close. There were more sounds. She heard the snapping of twigs, as if something was stepping on the leaves and twigs that lay on the ground.

Luvee's heart was pounding. This was the first time that she was confronting something on her own. She felt so alone.

She recognized the sound was coming from behind a big rock by the lake just ahead. "Maybe this exploring stuff isn't so great after all," she thought to herself. She didn't run away. She

stood by her decision to be strong and face what was out there making that noise. She was going to see what was out there, even if it meant her life might be
threatened.

Luvee Bunny's heart was pounding even faster! Then she reminded herself of her time with the Wise Ol' Owl. She had learned to become strong and had built up her bunny wisdom by talking with him, eating right and sleeping.

If she ran now, she will always wonder about this moment. Luvee Bunny decided to have the confidence and wisdom in herself in order to face this unfamiliar situation.

Luvee Bunny hopped ten steps forward, then two steps back. Then four steps forward and stood her ground. All those steps added up to a forward movement of twelve steps. Luvee had kept count. She would never forget her first twelve steps alone. The steps taken to face the future head on. She knew that her memory of these steps would give her strength within herself forever.

There was another snap of a branch behind the big rock. Luvee Bunny closed her eyes.

She opened her eyes to face her fears. It was the bravest thing a bunny could do.

She stared straight ahead. She remembered all she learned from the Wise Ol' Owl about making the right choice. She was ready.

There was a rustling noise, then a big furry leg stuck out from behind the rock, and then there was a great swift leap toward her, and...it was...she looked...but her eyes couldn't believe it...she couldn't believe...she never thought in a million years...it was...

Peter Rabbit!!!!!

It was really him!!!!

"Peter!" exclaimed Luvee Bunny!

"Luvee Bunny!" Peter shouted back! "You're here in an unknown pasture! How wonderful to see you!"

They grabbed each other's paws and danced about in a circle until they fell to the ground, laughing at first, and then just grinning, bunny ear to bunny ear.

Luvee Bunny said, "I finally left our home pasture so I could experience my first bunny story. But I never thought my first one would be you! What are you doing here?"

Peter said, " I have been out exploring many new pastures. Where else would I be?"

And at that, he laughed at his own words and Luvee Bunny laughed with him.

Peter's face grew serious. "The Wise Ol' Owl told me that one day soon there I would find the most important discovery of my life. I have been waiting and waiting for that day. Some wondrous things have happened to me on my journeys. I have seen beautiful sunrises and sunsets. I have smelled flowers that made me feel good for days and days. I have made so many different friends, but none of them felt quite special enough."

"Then, last night, the owl circled around me and told me that the answer I have been waiting for would be by the lake near this big rock. I hopped straight over. I slept here all night. I have been waiting for something to happen all day."

"I tried to think of ways to find this important discovery of my life the Wise Ol' Owl described. I have learned courage to change what I can change, accept what I cannot change, and the wisdom to know the difference. I fell into a nap this afternoon, and when I woke up, I thought of you. But out here, far from your home, I never imagined that you would decide to explore. I thought that I would have to spend my life exploring without you."

"But here you are." Peter hopped up to standing position. "I guess that owl really is smart. The day he told me that I would find the important discovery, I was telling him that if I had to live my life roaming, I would be fine. He asked me if I ever thought about you anymore. I told him I think about you every day. And then the Wise Ol' Owl asked, "What could be more important than spending your life with the bunny you love? What good is it to wander alone in this world?"

Peter Rabbit got down on one knee before Luvee Bunny.

"I love you, Luvee Bunny," Peter said. "Always have, always will." He took a deep breath before he continued.

"Luvee Bunny, would you be my wife and explore pastures with me forever?"

Luvee Bunny smiled as she never had before. "Oh, Peter! There is nothing else I want to do. I love you too, Peter Rabbit. Yes, yes, yes! I will marry you!"

As Peter and Luvee Bunny danced about again, Luvee Bunny cherished that this moment she was experiencing, would have never happened unless she faced her fears and took those first twelve steps.

She also knew it was time to focus and forge ahead. Where she came from and what she once did were experiences to be remembered. Life is to be lived from the present forward, not in the pain of the past or fear of the future. She knew where she was now and what she wanted. Living in the present moment would lead her to make wise choices of how to live her life.

As she and Peter now held paws, Luvee Bunny understood the future was only as scary as she allowed it to be. For once she envisioned hope in her future. She knew she was able to seek all that life had to offer and make the right choices with her bunny wisdom.

Both bunnies turned and hopped away

together. They would now have each other to create their bunny stories together.

Love always finds its way. It may take some time. But there is no stopping true love, there is no stopping the love between two creatures who insist on finding their way in the world....together.

Especially Luvee Bunny and Peter Rabbit.........

This story is dedicated to the most inspirational person on this earth, Layne Mary.....may the pastures that we experience together be the most wondrous journey that two bunnies could experience.

ABOUT THE AUTHOR

Chief Peter Volkmann, MSW, graduated with a Bachelor of Science in Criminal Justice from Mercy College and received his Master's in Social Work from Fordham University. He is a faculty member for the International Critical Incident Stress Foundation (ICISF) in Ellicott City, MD. In 2017, he received the ICISF Lifetime Achievement Award for his accomplishments in Critical Incident Stress Management.

Peter has over 30 years in law enforcement and served as a police officer and EMT in Peekskill NY, Town of Ossining NY, Town of Stockport NY, and is now the Chief of Police in Chatham NY. Peter developed the Chatham Cares 4 U Program in which his police agency has assisted over 200 people find treatment for their substance use disorder. He has testified to the NYS Assembly and NYS Senate pertaining to the opioid crisis facing our communities. Peter received the 2018 Police Assisted Addiction Recovery Initiative (PAARI) Leadership award for his accomplishments in the opioid crisis. In 2018, Peter was invited and attended the White House "Best Practices in Combatting the Opioid Epidemic Conference".

Peter is a person in long term recovery and lives in Columbia County NY with his wife and children.

ABOUT THE ILLUSTRATOR

Jaycee Layne Volkmann is a graduate student at The Sage Colleges and is currently completing her Master's degree in the accelerated, graduate Occupational Therapy Program. She was a collegiate athlete in soccer and basketball for Sage during her undergraduate studies. Jaycee has worked with developmentally disabled persons throughout her high school and college career. Jaycee is not only a gifted athlete, but she is also talented in her artistic expressions.

Made in the USA
Middletown, DE
15 March 2019